MW00973196

Rainbow's Landing

Written by Steve Tiller

Illustrated by Robert Cremeans

MichaelsMind LLC™

ATLANTA

Steve Tiller, Author
Robert Cremeans, Illustrator / Creative Director
Kathryn L. Tecosky, Editor
Rich Tecosky, Research

Special thanks to: Our Families; CCAD; Fred Harris and June Vickers; Mark Wynns; David
and Melissa Abbey at Abbey Design, Jim and Stacy Scott, Richard Williams, and
Brian Bias our Apple Guru. Special special thanks to Janet, Katie, Rachel, Ben, Holly,
Naomi, Blue, and Noah for all the help they give to us everyday. You are all a continuing
source of material uh, inspiration.

Library of Congress Cataloging-in-Publication Data
Tiller, Steve
Summary: Life on the reef with a clownfish and a sea anemone

ISBN 0-9704597-5-0
[1. Fish-Fiction.   2. Underwater-Fiction.   3. Stories with Fish]

First printing, July 2001
Printed by Daehan Printing, South Korea

Look for these other books by MichaelsMind: Tangle Fairies, Connected at the Heart,
Rainbow's Landing and Henry Hump's Born to Fly

Illustrations in this book were created on a Macintosh G4 computer using Adobe Photoshop.

To: The Fred and Lucy Harris Family; to the Tallahassee
Group- my home away from home; to my son Ben whom I
always enjoy; and to the Paradise Father who gives us form,
substance and meaning.

— S.T.

To: Honeychild, Little One & Frosty XOXOXO

— R.C.

"Freddie!!" Lucy the clownfish cried joyfully as she dove into a mass of waving purple tentacles.

 Those tentacles belonged to Fred. Lucy thought Fred was the most handsome sea anemone in Rainbow's Landing. Fred was Lucy's closest friend. She loved to tell the news from the reef, and Fred loved to hear it.

"What did you see today?" Fred's eager voice floated to the sharp ears of the clownfish.

"I saw a baby ray burrowing into the sand. It was so cute with its black eyes peeping out. And you should see Sara Sponge's new children. She is such a proud mom!"

Fred loved his life on the reef, but he had a secret dream. He wanted to follow the tide and see the fantastic fish, colorful crabs, and slithering squids in the open sea.

"Just once," sighed Fred to himself. "It's not fair, that I am stuck on this rock!" he complained loudly to Lucy.

"Cheer up, your time will come!" the little clownfish would assure her friend. Fred would soon smile as Lucy told him of her adventures on the reef.

"I saw the most fantastic lionfish," she chuckled, "The moray eel came charging out of his hole to scare him like he does with all the little fish, but that big lionfish just darted right up to the old eel. Boy, did that eel slink back into his hole fast."

Fred always got a nervous feeling in the pit of his stomach whenever he heard about the moray eel. "You be careful around that eel, Lucy. He has a mean temper."

"Don't worry" replied Lucy, "that old eel is way too slow to ever catch me!"

Fred and Lucy would talk about their neighbors on the beautiful reef until the late night stars danced in the sky above the sea.

Fred and Lucy lived in a small village on the reef called Rainbow's Landing. Captain Rainbow had founded the colony of sea anemones and was loved by everyone. Everybody just called him Captain.

Fred loved the Captain's laughter and his long flowing yellow and green tentacles. Captain Rainbow was very wise. Next to Lucy, the old sea Captain was Fred's best friend. Fred and the Captain would talk for hours about Rainbow's Landing.

"Forming a village takes time. We all have to work together," Captain Rainbow would say, "and we have to recognize the talents of each and every one of us."

"But just what are my talents?" asked Fred.

The old sea Captain stared into Fred's eyes and smiled to himself. "Time will tell Fred, but I think you may be surprised."

Captain Rainbow saw Lucy speeding back and forth across the reef and a big smile broke across his face.

"You might even surprise Lucy, and not much surprises her! Take it easy on yourself, Fred, sometimes the very thing we think is our biggest problem turns out to be our greatest gift."

"Captain, my biggest problem is something I can't do anything about. I am stuck to this reef. I want to travel the open sea, but wishing won't make that dream come true."

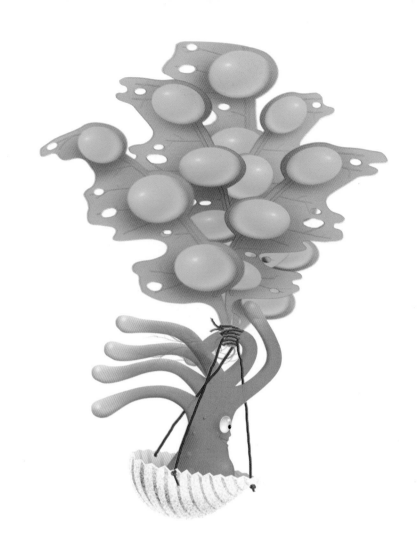

The Captain looked at his young friend and announced confidently, "Dreams do come true! Life can change with the tide. But when those changes come we have to have the courage to let those changes take us to our dreams."

"I don't think I can make this dream come true, Captain," Fred's discouraged voice floated quietly on the waves.

"Have faith, Freddie. If you can dare to dream it, the Great Sea can make it come true! When the time is right you will know."

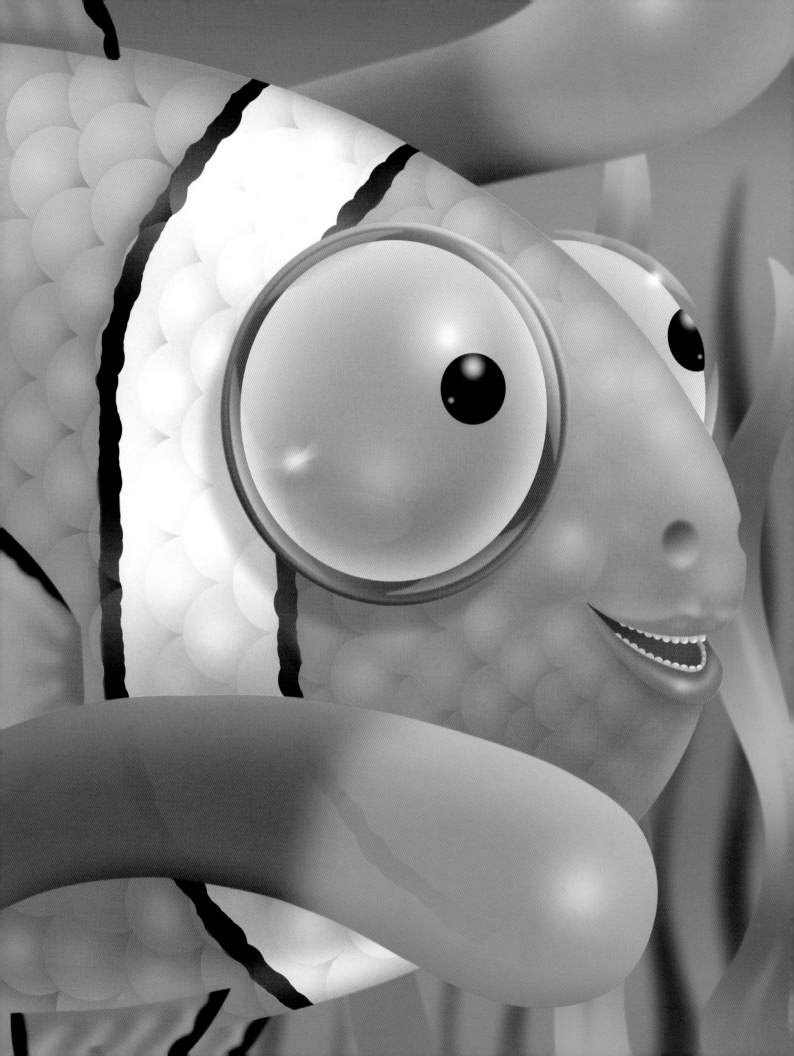

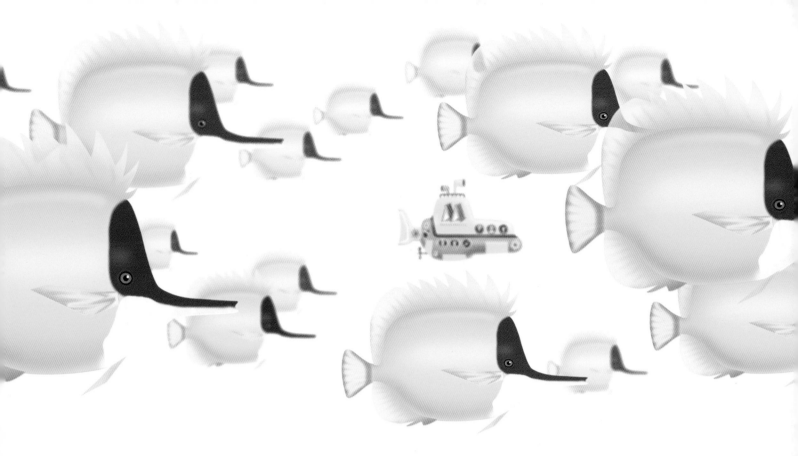

"Hello, Captain Rainbow!" shouted Lucy as she dove toward them.

"Hello back! Lucy Clownfish!" called the Captain.

"I was just telling Freddie that he needs to trust himself and to trust his dreams!"

"I have been telling him that myself!" she giggled.

"I know, I know," said Fred smiling back at Lucy.

"Choose your path..." Captain Rainbow began one of his famous sayings.

"Ride the tide, and dig in deep!" said all three finishing together with a laugh.

Time passed comfortably on the colorful reef. The Captain and Fred had many long talks. Lucy explored every day and brought back news of all the wonders she found in the deep blue seas around Rainbow's Landing.

One day a large storm struck. The waves crashed over the shallow reef uprooting sea lilies, bashing sponges, and sending fish swirling away from its shelter. The sea anemones of Captain Rainbow's little village were hanging on for dear life!

Fred felt his grip on the reef begin to break loose from the jolt of the crashing waves. He was terrified and he clutched at the ledge.

Suddenly a calm voice spoke quietly in his mind, "This is your time. Let go and follow your dreams!" Fred's excitement mounted. In that moment Fred knew he could leave the safety of the rocky ledge and find adventure in the open sea. Each wave bent him back further and further. As his courage grew a large wave crashed over him. The strain of the Great Sea tugged against him. Fred knew he could twist free. Thrill and fear surged through him with each pull of the tide. He heard Captain Rainbow's strong and steady voice above the storm.

"Freddie, there is not much time. Remember, choose your path, ride the tide, and dig in deep!"

All at once Fred was ripped free from the reef. His heart pounded. His mouth was dry. But his mind was crystal clear. Debris from the storm was everywhere. He could see an open path and he let the tide pull him toward it.

"Lucy!" Fred called into the storm. "I'm free! Follow me if you can!" He didn't hear an answer, but he knew Lucy was always nearby. Fred rode the wave as it pulled him along the open sea. Even with the fury of the storm, it was thrilling to be free. He could see the most fantastic shapes. Gigantic sponges shaped like wondrous horns on imaginary dragons rushed past. Colossal fan corals whipped from side to side in the pulling tide.

The current towed him past two towers like ancient guards standing between the ridges of the reef. Fred's fear changed to a sense of wonder. Fish soared past the rubble of the passing storm. Fred slipped under a huge Stingray

with vast fins surfing the storm tide. The current pulled Fred
back and forth driving him toward a drab vertical wall where
no living thing was seen. He could hear Lucy shouting at
him, but he was too far away to understand her.

Suddenly out from a crack in the rocks darted wicked yellow eyes and enormous teeth. Panic flooded Fred as the cruel mouth shot out of the rocky ridge to tear him apart. Out of the corner of his eye he saw Lucy flying toward the blind side of moray eel. She hit him in the back of his yellow eye. The moray flinched and the snapping jaws missed. The surf surged again and Fred streamed past the stabbing teeth of the nasty eel. Fred was shaking with fear. He turned just in time to see the eel's mouth open wide, the wicked teeth slam shut, and Lucy disappear.

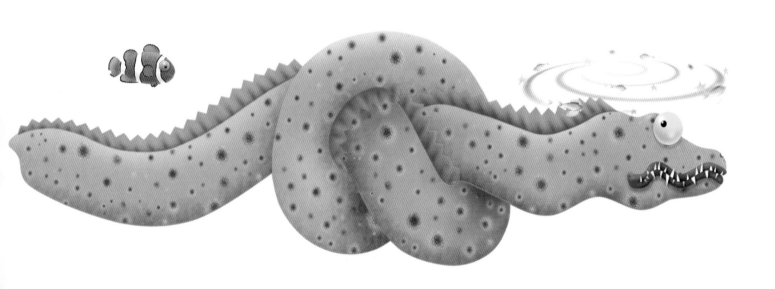

Fred feared Lucy was lost forever. He had never felt so alone. Fred was tired, and he was afraid. He watched carefully. He saw a ledge up ahead. Fred chose his path. The current flowed and he rode the tide toward the rocky ledge. As he came into reach of the reef, he dug himself into a shallow crack. The sea tried to pull him back. He fought the tide and gripped the ledge. The surge passed leaving him in place. The next wave hit him but he held on. Another wave came, and another. Fred dug in deep.

"The Captain wasn't kidding about digging in deep!" mumbled Fred wearily to himself.

The fight to grip the reef left him exhausted. Fred groaned when he thought of Lucy. "How did I let this happen?" he asked himself. Slowly the storm passed, and the waves rocked Fred to sleep.

When Fred awoke, he looked around for Lucy until he remembered the battle with the eel. Fred could see Rainbow's Landing on a ledge across the reef. He was a very long way from home. A great sense of sadness swept across him.

Fred saw Captain Rainbow's long colorful tentacles waving at him. Then suddenly out of nowhere, shot a familiar streak of orange and white.

"Lucy!" Fred's heart leapt with joy.

"Freddie!" Lucy cheered.

Fred was amazed. "How did you get away? I saw him eat you!"

Lucy took a little bow. "Eat me? Not likely," she giggled, "I told you I was way too fast for that old eel. Sometimes I swim though his teeth just to warm up in the morning! Boy, are you a mess! But I will have you cleaned up in no time! The Captain sends his regards!" Lucy told her friend. "He said he knew you would fulfill your dreams."

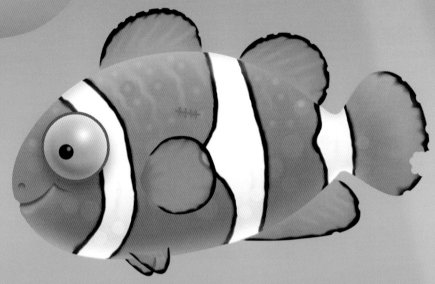

Fred looked surprised. What do you mean? I haven't fulfilled any dreams. I got torn off Rainbow's Landing."

"You dreamed of exploring the sea." Lucy reminded him.

"Well, yes but,..."

"The Great Sea made it possible," Lucy said firmly, "Dreams don't always turn out exactly like we think you know!".

"But I didn't want to get stuck here!" Fred pointed out.

"You are not stuck! Captain Rainbow is so proud of you. You had the courage to follow your dream when the time came. Now you will be your own Captain and begin a new village of your own!"

Fred was stunned for a minute. "A Captain? Me?" He looked around at the ledge where he landed. "Start my own village?"

He looked across the shallow pools toward Rainbow's Landing. Finally, all the long talks with the Captain made sense. Fred chuckled. He looked back toward the dancing tentacles of Captain Rainbow. They seemed to congratulate him. Fred's grip on the reef grew more solid. This rock was his own!

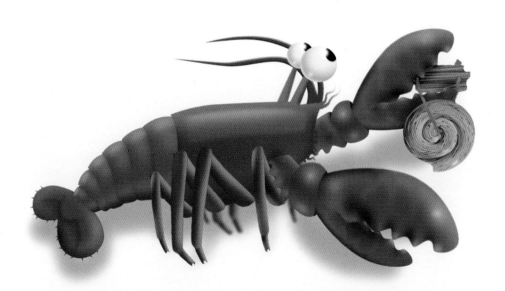

"The Captain did have one question he wanted me to ask," Lucy said mischievously.

"What are you going to call your new home? He told me to tell you the name Rainbow's Landing is already taken."

For the first time Fred understood that once upon a time a young Captain Rainbow had dreamed his own dreams, chose his own path, and had taken his own ride on the tide.

Fred smiled proudly as he looked at his new home, "Go tell the Captain I said *Fred's Ledge* is up and running!"

MichaelsMind LLC

THE END

Parker Bomar

Mia Bomar

Katie Brewster

Special thanks to the Children and Families who participated in the HIES silent auction 2001

Steve Tiller was always accused of circular thinking by his teachers. He was never exactly sure what they meant,

or whether it was a compliment. But it does seem to him he is always arriving back at his departure point.

Steve lives in Atlanta with his two girls Katie and Rachel. His son Ben lives on his own close by and is a frequent and always

welcome visitor. His mother, Janet, also of Atlanta, is a fan and supporter. There is a saying that nuts do not fall far from the

tree. His family may be emulating this astute philosophical proposition. He hopes so. He likes the nuts around his tree.

Husband, Daddy, and "Computer Folk Artist" **Robert Cremeans** was born and raised in Huntington, West Virginia.

He lives in Lawrenceville, Georgia, with his lovely wife, Naomi; beautiful daughter, Blue; and wonderful son, Noah. His career

as an illustrator began shortly after he graduated with a B.F.A. from Columbus College of Art and Design.

He became the luckiest man alive the day he met Naomi.

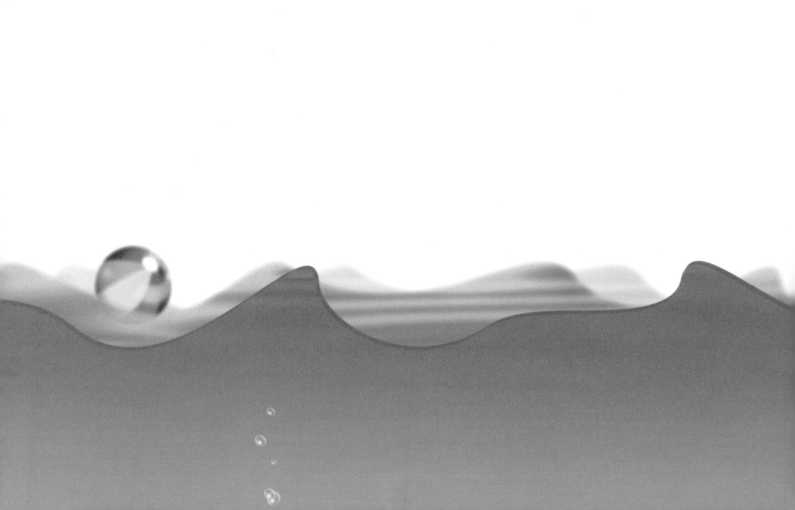